Dear Parents:

Congratulations! Your child is taking
the first steps on an exciting journey.
The destination? Independent reading!

STEP INTO READING® will help your child get there. The program offers
five steps to reading success. Each step includes fun stories and colorful
art or photographs. In addition to original fiction and books with favorite
characters, there are Step into Reading Non-Fiction Readers, Phonics Readers
and Boxed Sets, Sticker Readers, and Comic Readers—a complete literacy
program with something to interest every child.

Learning to Read, Step by Step!

Ready to Read   Preschool–Kindergarten
• big type and easy words • rhyme and rhythm • picture clues
For children who know the alphabet and are eager to
begin reading.

Reading with Help   Preschool–Grade 1
• basic vocabulary • short sentences • simple stories
For children who recognize familiar words and sound out
new words with help.

Reading on Your Own   Grades 1–3
• engaging characters • easy-to-follow plots • popular topics
For children who are ready to read on their own.

Reading Paragraphs   Grades 2–3
• challenging vocabulary • short paragraphs • exciting stories
For newly independent readers who read simple sentences
with confidence.

Ready for Chapters   Grades 2–4
• chapters • longer paragraphs • full-color art
For children who want to take the plunge into chapter books
but still like colorful pictures.

STEP INTO READING® is designed to give every child a successful
reading experience. The grade levels are only guides; children will progress
through the steps at their own speed, developing confidence in their reading.
The F&P Text Level on the back cover serves as another tool to help you
choose the right book for your child.

Remember, a lifetime love of reading starts with a single step!

For Molly Rose DeVries and
all her friends!
—D.H.
To Jan
—S.W.

Text copyright © 2003 by Deborah Hautzig
Cover art and interior illustrations copyright © 2003 by Sylvie Wickstrom
All rights reserved. Published in the United States by Random House Children's Books, a
division of Penguin Random House LLC, New York.
Step into Reading, Random House, and the Random House colophon are registered
trademarks of Penguin Random House LLC.

Visit us on the Web!
StepIntoReading.com
randomhousekids.com

Educators and librarians, for a variety of teaching tools, visit us at
RHTeachersLibrarians.com

Library of Congress Cataloging-in-Publication Data
Hautzig, Deborah.
Little Witch learns to read / by Deborah Hautzig ; illustrated by Sylvie Wickstrom.
   p. cm. — (Step into reading. A step 3 book)
Summary: Little Witch's family is not at all helpful when she is learning to read, so she hides
her books and reads by flashlight until late at night and becomes so sleepy that she cannot stay
awake during the day.
ISBN 978-0-375-82179-0 (trade) — ISBN 978-0-375-92179-7 (lib. bdg.)
[1. Witches—Fiction. 2. Books and reading—Fiction. 3. Schools—Fiction.
4. Family life—Fiction.] I. Wickstrom, Sylvie, ill. II. Title. III. Series: Step into reading. Step 3
book.   PZ7.H2888 Ligk 2003 [E]—dc21 2002152691

Printed in the United States of America 18 17 16 15 14 13 12 11 10 9

This book has been officially leveled by using the F&P Text Level Gradient™ Leveling System.

STEP INTO READING®

STEP 3
READING ON YOUR OWN

Little Witch Learns to Read

by Deborah Hautzig
illustrated by Sylvie Wickstrom

Random House New York

Little Witch loved school.

She loved making art projects.

She loved science.

She loved to feed the gerbil,
Mr. Coffee.

Most of all, she loved
learning to read.

Her teacher's name was
Ms. Brooks.
Little Witch worked hard.
She learned to sound out
new words.
Some words were called
"sight words," like "night"
and "friend."
"These are words you
have to remember
just by looking at them,"
said Ms. Brooks.
And slowly, Little Witch did.

"Read a book every night
with your mommy or daddy,"
Ms. Brooks told the class.
"They can read to you.
And soon you will be able
to read to THEM!"

Ms. Brooks took the class
to the school library
every week.
"You may borrow any book
for a week.
When you return it,
you may borrow another one!"

That night, Little Witch

asked Mother Witch

to read to her.

"No!" screamed Mother Witch.

"Bedtime stories are

for children—not witches!

Get rid of that book!"

WITCHES WEAR

Next, Little Witch asked
Cousin Dippy to read to her.
Cousin Dippy was happy
to do it!
But she mixed up all the words.
"Came tulip lovely thumb girl,"
read Cousin Dippy.

Little Witch sighed.

"Never mind, Cousin Dippy."

Little Witch asked

Aunt Nasty to read to her.

"Once upon a time,

I gave rotten fish to a cat.

He threw up on my head!"

said Aunt Nasty.

"EW!" said Little Witch.

"That is not what the book says!

That is about YOU!"

Aunt Nasty and Aunt Grouchy

giggled wickedly.

"I cannot WAIT
until I can read
all by myself!"
Little Witch told her cat,
Bow-Wow.

She tried to read by herself.

She read some of the words,

but not all of them.

"Well, some is better than none,"

she said to her bat, Scrubby.

Then she put away her book

and went to sleep.

The next morning, Mother Witch
warned Little Witch.
"Remember—
NO NICE BOOKS
allowed in this house!"

Little Witch went
to the library.
She had an idea.
"I will borrow a book
and hide it with a magic spell.
Mother Witch will never know!"
Little Witch checked out
The Little Mermaid
and put it in her backpack.

As soon as she got home,

Little Witch ran to her room

and said a magic spell:

"Lingo bingo,

Wordy itch,

Hide yourself

From Mother Witch!"

POOF!

The book disappeared.

Little Witch peeked
under her bed,
and there it was.
"She'll never find it here!
Mother Witch NEVER cleans
my room."

Later that night,

all the witches were in bed.

Little Witch turned on

her flashlight.

She snuggled up with her book

and tried to read.

Soon it was midnight!

Bow-Wow was fast asleep.

Scrubby was wide awake.

But Little Witch could not

keep her eyes open

one second longer.

The next morning,

Little Witch overslept!

"WAKE UP!" screamed

Mother Witch.

"Why are you still sleeping?"

Mother Witch stamped her foot.

Little Witch was sleepy all day.

She fell asleep at her desk . . .

in the lunchroom . . .

and even playing hopscotch.

Ms. Brooks was worried.

Little Witch began
staying up late
every night reading.
But she was getting
more and more sleepy every day.

Little Witch tried a magic spell:
"Jumpity lumpity,
Coffee shake,
Help me, PLEASE,
To stay awake!"

The spell did not work.

She even fell asleep at dinner.

Mother Witch was worried.
The witches had a meeting
while Little Witch was
at school.
"Little Witch is so sleepy,"
said Mother Witch.
"We have to find out why."

They looked for clues.

They searched the yard.

They searched the whole house.

At last they came
to Little Witch's room.
Mother Witch looked
under the bed.
"AHA!" she screeched,
and pulled out a book.

"White Snow," read
Cousin Dippy. . . .
"I thought ALL snow was white!"
"That's backward,"
said Mother Witch.
"It's called *Snow White*."

They read the first page.

Then they read the last page—

"'And they lived

happily ever after.'"

"AAAAAHHHHHHHH!!!!"

screamed Mother Witch.

"What is this nice book doing

in OUR HOUSE?"

When Little Witch came home,
all the witches were waiting.

Mother Witch

waved the book in her face.

"WHY WAS THIS BOOK

UNDER YOUR BED?"

she screamed.

Little Witch hung her head.

"I learned to read at school,"
she said.

"I love hearing stories.
But nobody will read them
to me!
So I read them to myself."

"But this book is terrible!"
wailed Mother Witch.
"It's all about a lovely princess
who lives happily ever after!"

"But, Mother Witch,

didn't you read about

the poison apple?

And the evil queen?

And the ugly old witch?"

"Oooooh," gasped Aunt Nasty

and Aunt Grouchy.

"Evil! Witches! Poison! Yum!"

"Really?" asked Mother Witch.

"Really," said Little Witch.

That night, everyone sat together
in the family room.
Little Witch read aloud.
"And the evil queen said,
'Take Snow White into the forest
and kill her,'" read Little Witch.

The witches rubbed
their bony hands together
and giggled.

"Keep reading!"
said Aunt Grouchy.

Then Little Witch read
the part about the prince.
But Aunt Grouchy
and Aunt Nasty
were fast asleep.

"What's a prince?"

asked Cousin Dippy.

"There are none!"

said Mother Witch.

"Be quiet and let

Little Witch finish!"

And Little Witch did.

Mother Witch put Little Witch
to bed.

"That book has a
very stupid ending.
Nobody lives happily ever after!
But the middle parts
were good."

"Do you think I am

a good reader?"

asked Little Witch.

"Yes," said Mother Witch.

"You are good at everything—

except being BAD!"

The next morning,
Little Witch woke up early.
She wasn't sleepy at all!
She put *Snow White*
in her backpack.
"Bring home another book,"
said Mother Witch.
"But only if it is wicked."

"It's a deal," said Little Witch
with a wink.
Mother Witch gave Little Witch
a big hug.
Then Little Witch flew
off to school.